THE PRIDE
Chapter One

BRIAN K. VAUGHAN writer **ADRIAN ALPHONA** penciler **DAVID NEWBOLD** inker
BRIAN REBER colorist **JO CHEN** cover artist **PAUL TUTRONE** letterer **STEPHANIE MOORE** asst. editor
C.B. CEBULSKI editor **JOE QUESADA** chief **BILL JEMAS** president

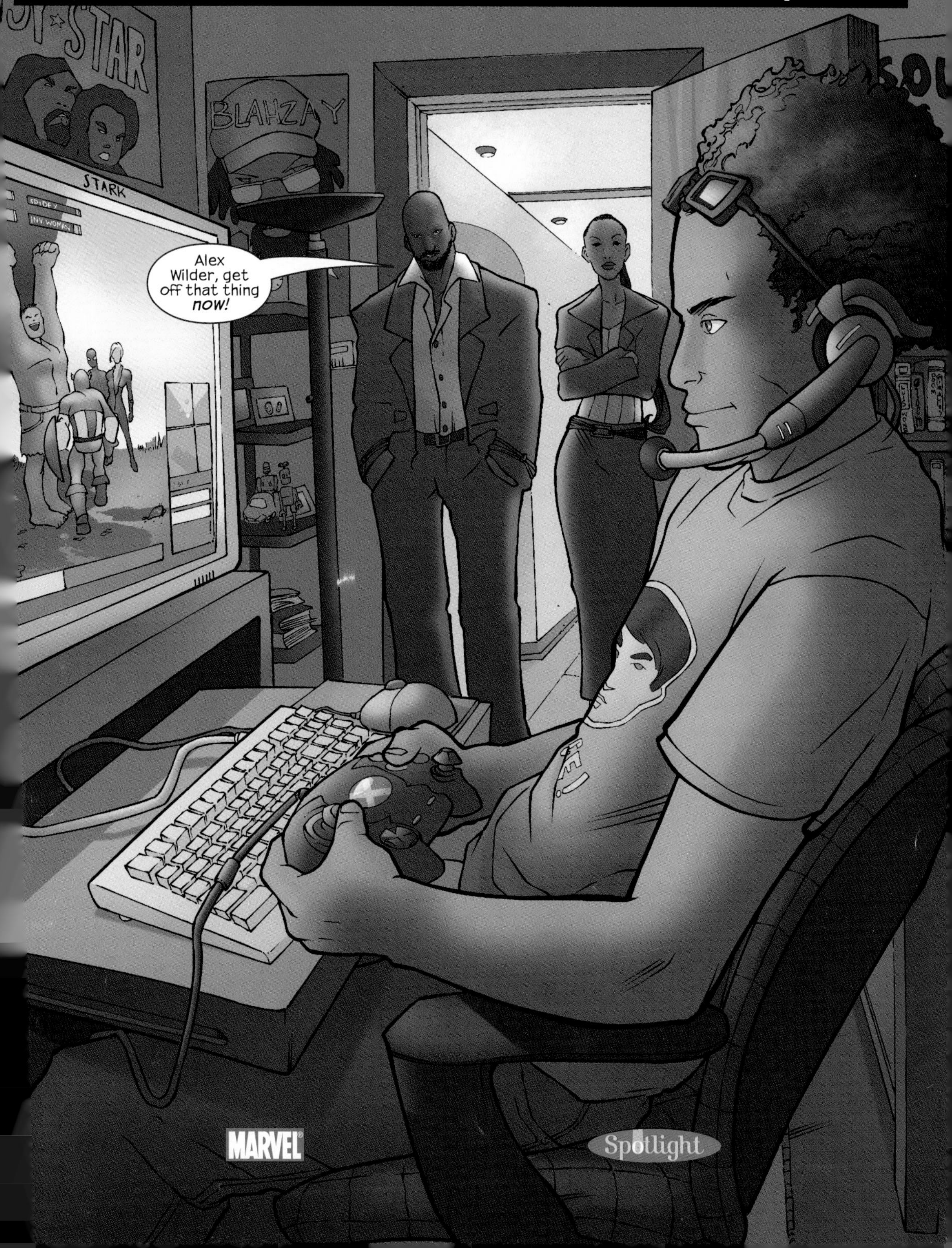
STAR
BLAHZAY
STARK
SPIDEY
INV. WOMAN
Alex Wilder, get off that thing *NOW!*
MARVEL
Spotlight

VISIT US AT
www.abdopublishing.com

Reinforced library bound edition published in 2007 by Spotlight, a division of the ABDO Publishing Group, Edina, Minnesota. Spotlight produces high-quality reinforced library bound editions for schools and libraries. Published by agreement with Marvel Characters, Inc.

Library of Congress Cataloging-in-Publication Data

Vaughan, Brian K.
   Runaways / [Brian K. Vaughan, writer ; Adrian Alphona, penciler].
     v. cm.
   Cover title.
   Revisions of issues 1-6 of the serial Runaways.
   "Marvel Age."
   Contents: #1. The pride -- #2. Running -- #3. Hidden powers -- #4. A new friend -- #5. Rescue mission -- #6. The hostel.
   ISBN-13: 978-1-59961-293-5 (v. 1)
   ISBN-10: 1-59961-293-3 (v. 1)
   ISBN-13: 978-1-59961-294-2 (v. 2)
   ISBN-10: 1-59961-294-1 (v. 2)
   ISBN-13: 978-1-59961-295-9 (v. 3)
   ISBN-10: 1-59961-295-X (v. 3)
   ISBN-13: 978-1-59961-296-6 (v. 4)
   ISBN-10: 1-59961-296-8 (v. 4)
   ISBN-13: 978-1-59961-297-3 (v. 5)
   ISBN-10: 1-59961-297-6 (v. 5)
   ISBN-13: 978-1-59961-298-0 (v. 6)
   ISBN-10: 1-59961-298-4 (v. 6)
    1. Comic books, strips, etc. I. Alphona, Adrian. II. Title. III. Title: Pride. IV. Title: Running. V. Title: Hidden powers. VI. Title: New friend. VII. Title: Rescue mission. VIII. Title: Hostel.

PN6728.R865V38 2007
791.5'73--dc22

2006050629

All Spotlight books are reinforced library binding
and manufactured in the United States of America.

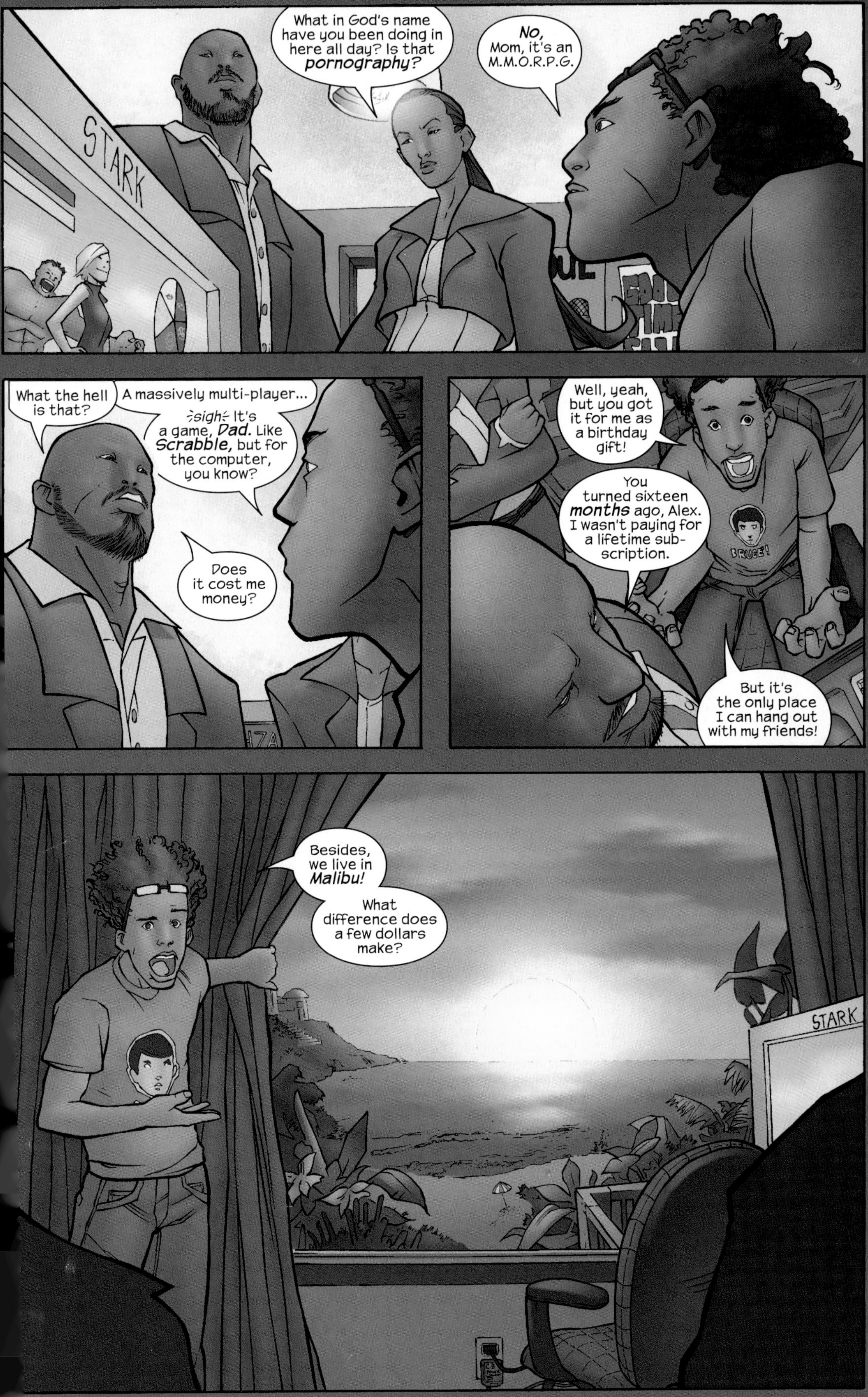
What in God's name have you been doing in here all day? Is that pornography?
No, Mom, it's an M.M.O.R.P.G.
STARK
What the hell is that?
A massively multi-player...
-sigh- It's a game, Dad. Like Scrabble, but for the computer, you know?
Does it cost me money?
Well, yeah, but you got it for me as a birthday gift!
You turned sixteen months ago, Alex. I wasn't paying for a lifetime sub-scription.
But it's the only place I can hang out with my friends!
Besides, we live in Malibu!
What difference does a few dollars make?
STARK

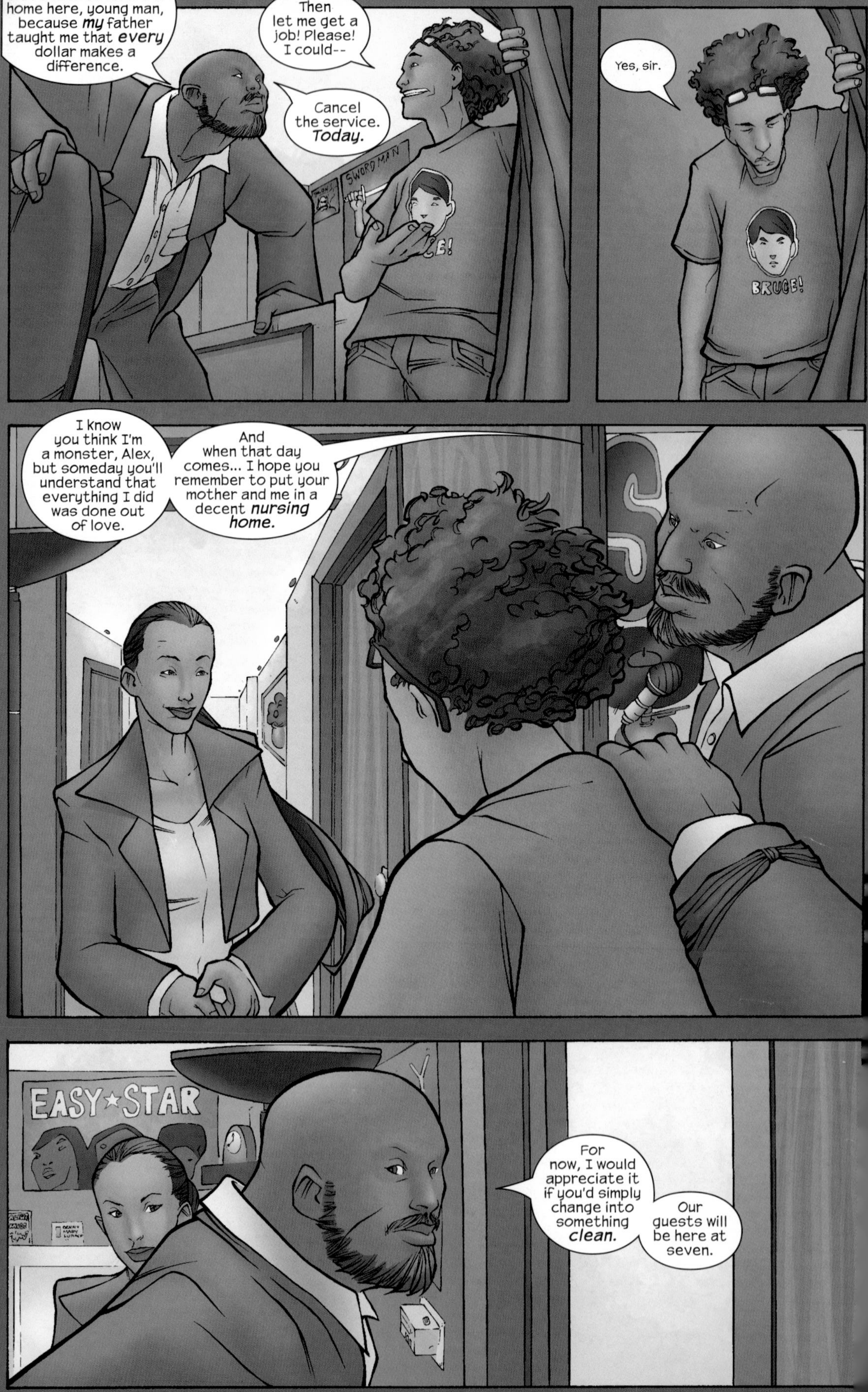
We're able to afford a home here, young man, because *my* father taught me that *every* dollar makes a difference.
Then let me get a job! Please! I could--
Cancel the service. *Today.*
SWORD MAN
BRUCE!
Yes, sir.
BRUCE!
I know you think I'm a monster, Alex, but someday you'll understand that everything I did was done out of love.
And when that day comes... I hope you remember to put your mother and me in a decent *nursing home.*
EASY★STAR
For now, I would appreciate it if you'd simply change into something *clean.*
Our guests will be here at seven.

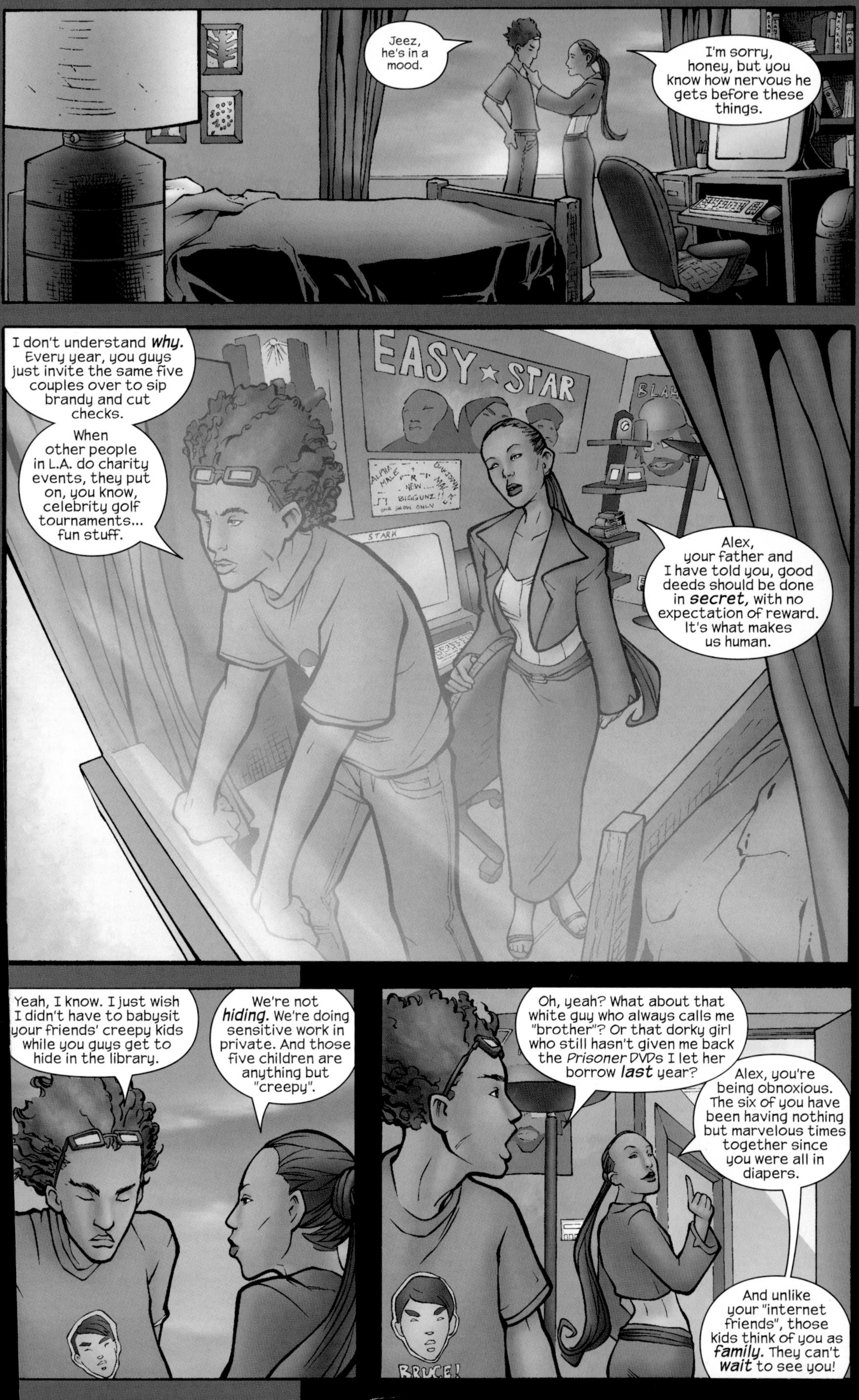
Jeez, he's in a mood.
I'm sorry, honey, but you know how nervous he gets before these things.
EASY ★ STAR
I don't understand *why.* Every year, you guys just invite the same five couples over to sip brandy and cut checks.
When other people in L.A. do charity events, they put on, you know, celebrity golf tournaments... fun stuff.
STARK
Alex, your father and I have told you, good deeds should be done in *secret,* with no expectation of reward. It's what makes us human.
Yeah, I know. I just wish I didn't have to babysit your friends' creepy kids while you guys get to hide in the library.
We're not *hiding.* We're doing sensitive work in private. And those five children are anything but "creepy".
Oh, yeah? What about that white guy who always calls me "brother"? Or that dorky girl who still hasn't given me back the *Prisoner* DVDs I let her borrow *last* year?
Alex, you're being obnoxious. The six of you have been having nothing but marvelous times together since you were all in diapers.
And unlike your "internet friends", those kids think of you as *family.* They can't *wait* to see you!
BRUCE!

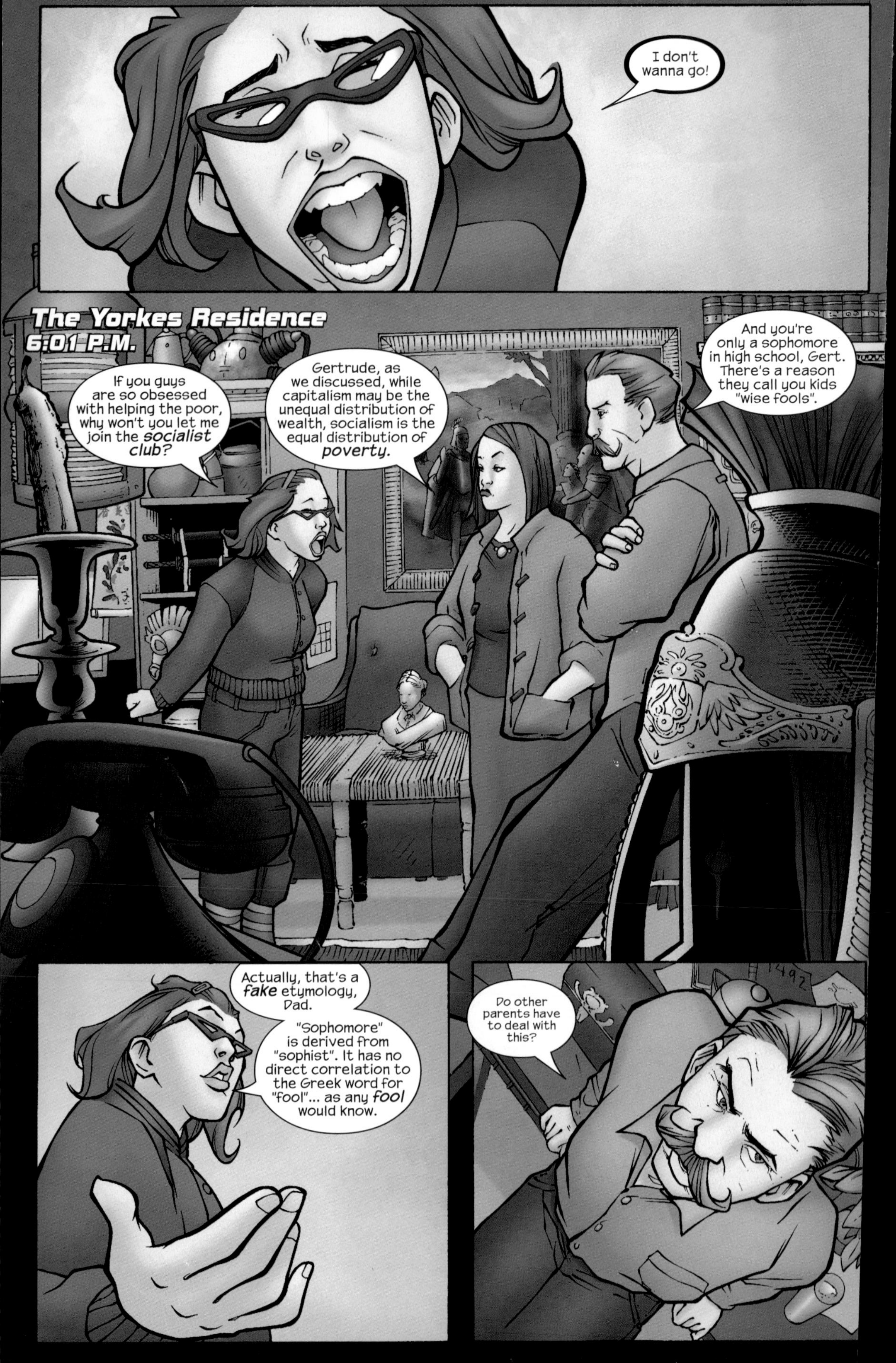

I don't wanna go!
The Yorkes Residence
6:01 P.M.
If you guys are so obsessed with helping the poor, why won't you let me join the socialist club?
Gertrude, as we discussed, while capitalism may be the unequal distribution of wealth, socialism is the equal distribution of poverty.
And you're only a sophomore in high school, Gert. There's a reason they call you kids "wise fools".
Actually, that's a fake etymology, Dad.
"Sophomore" is derived from "sophist". It has no direct correlation to the Greek word for "fool"... as any fool would know.
Do other parents have to deal with this?

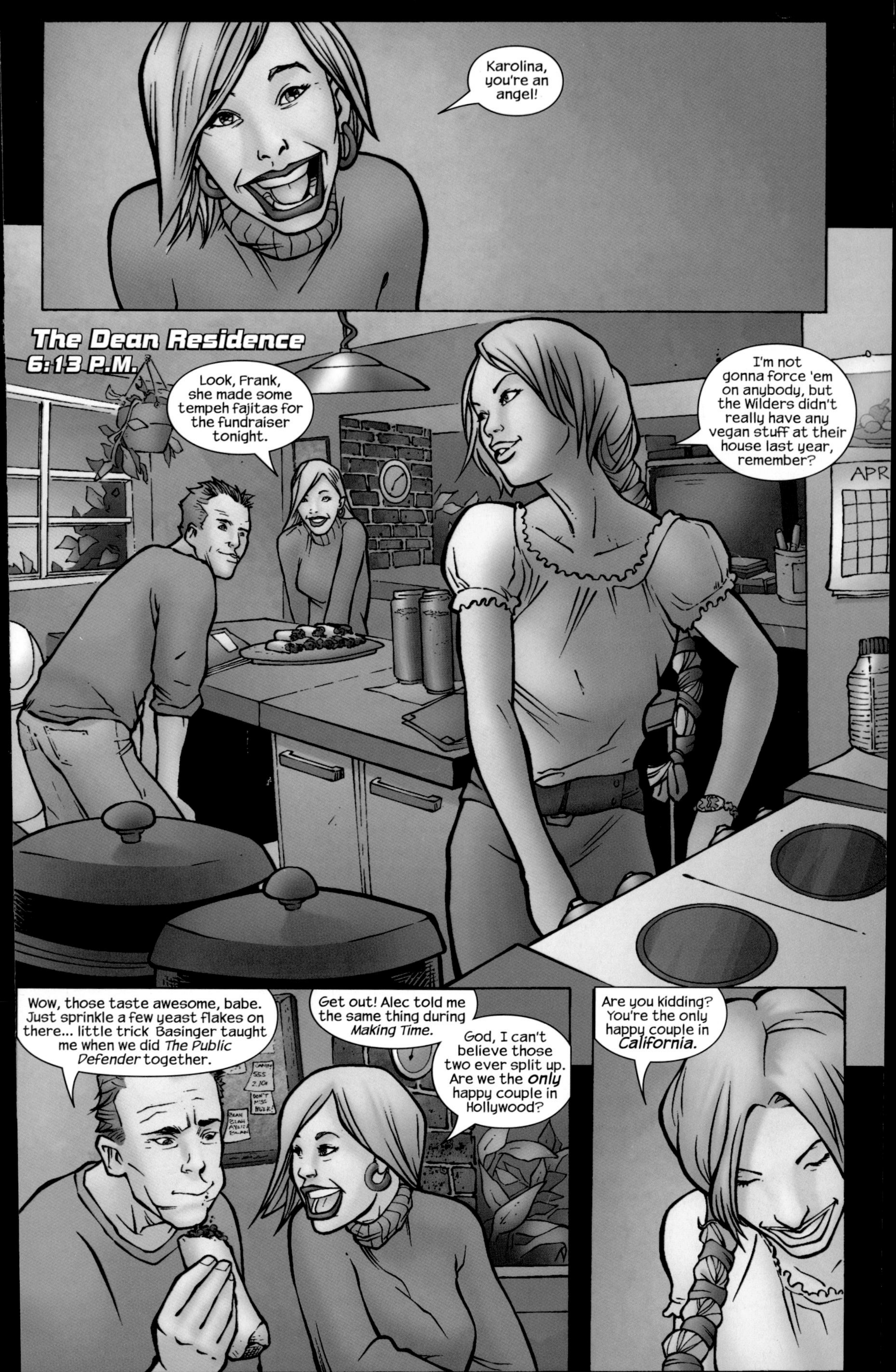
Karolina, you're an angel!
The Dean Residence
6:13 P.M.
Look, Frank, she made some tempeh fajitas for the fundraiser tonight.
I'm not gonna force 'em on anybody, but the Wilders didn't really have any vegan stuff at their house last year, remember?
APR
Wow, those taste awesome, babe. Just sprinkle a few yeast flakes on there... little trick Basinger taught me when we did *The Public Defender* together.
Get out! Alec told me the same thing during *Making Time.*
God, I can't believe those two ever split up. Are we the *only* happy couple in Hollywood?
Are you kidding? You're the only happy couple in *California.*

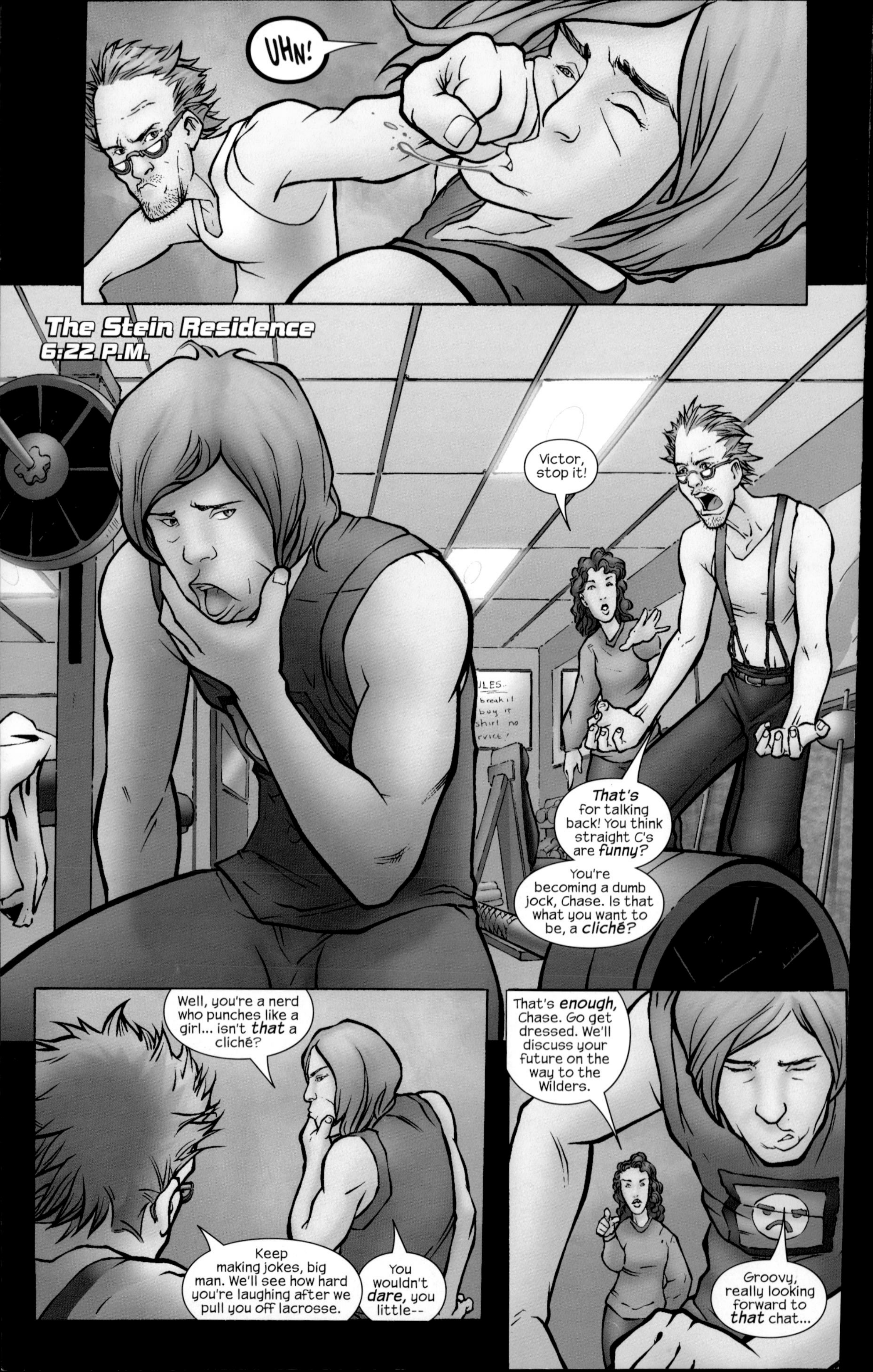
UHN!
The Stein Residence
6:22 P.M.
Victor, stop it!
That's for talking back! You think straight C's are funny?
You're becoming a dumb jock, Chase. Is that what you want to be, a cliché?
Well, you're a nerd who punches like a girl... isn't that a cliché?
Keep making jokes, big man. We'll see how hard you're laughing after we pull you off lacrosse.
You wouldn't dare, you little--
That's enough, Chase. Go get dressed. We'll discuss your future on the way to the Wilders.
Groovy, really looking forward to that chat...

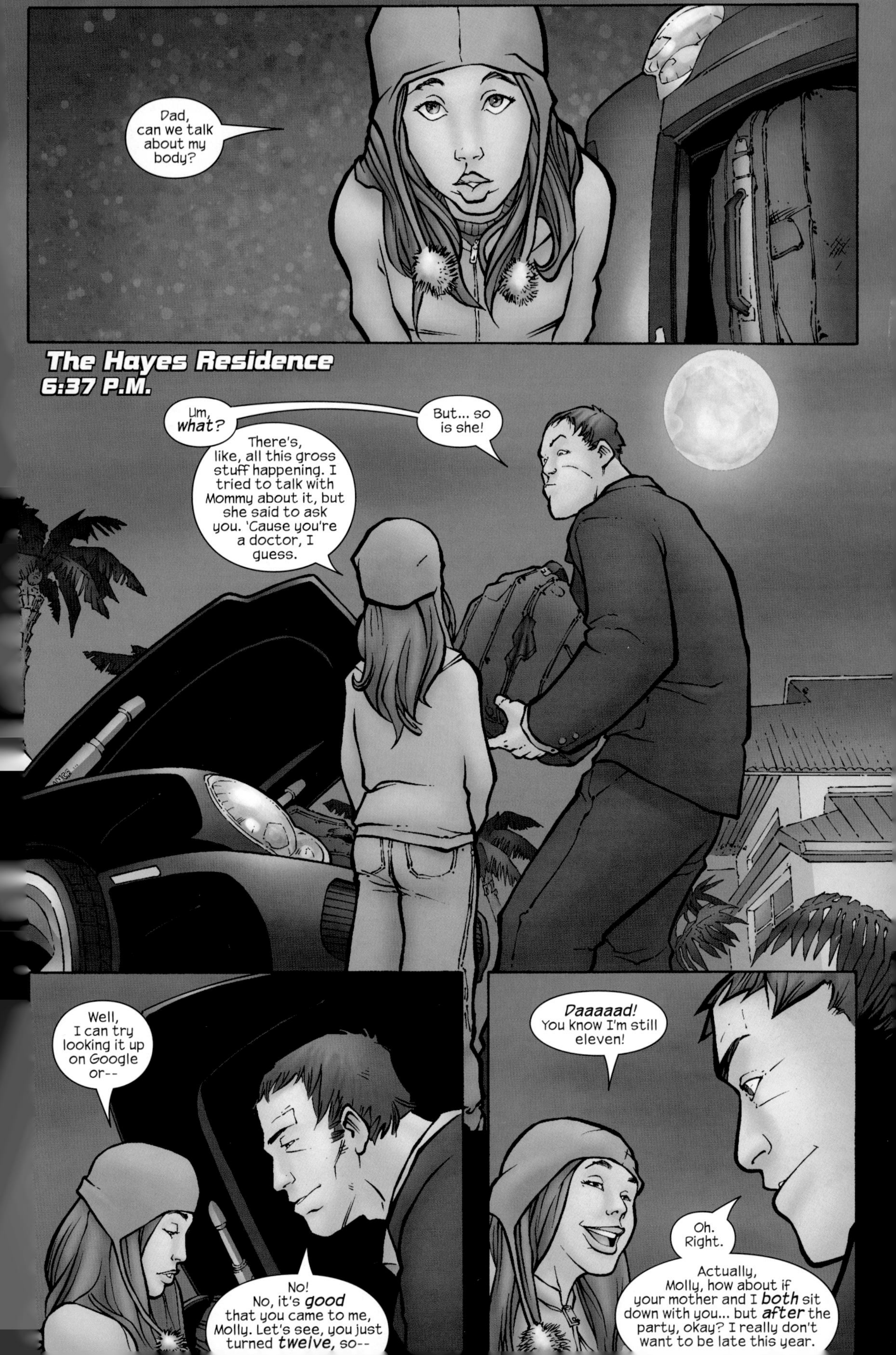

Dad, can we talk about my body?
The Hayes Residence
6:37 P.M.
Um, what?
There's, like, all this gross stuff happening. I tried to talk with Mommy about it, but she said to ask you. 'Cause you're a doctor, I guess.
But... so is she!
Well, I can try looking it up on Google or--
No! No, it's good that you came to me, Molly. Let's see, you just turned twelve, so--
Daaaaad! You know I'm still eleven!
Oh. Right.
Actually, Molly, how about if your mother and I both sit down with you... but after the party, okay? I really don't want to be late this year.

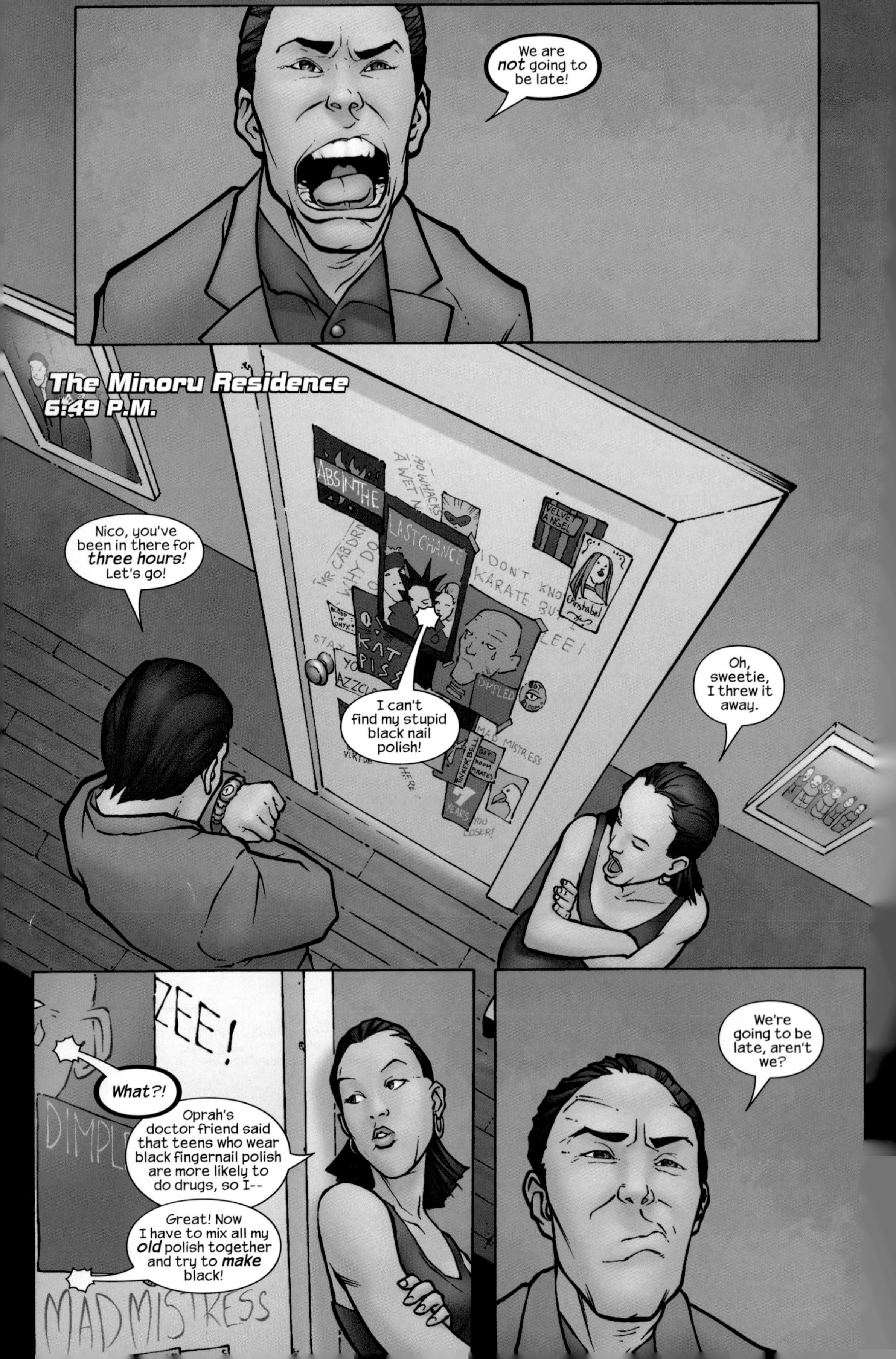

We are *not* going to be late!
The Minoru Residence
6:49 P.M.
Nico, you've been in there for *three hours!* Let's go!
I can't find my stupid black nail polish!
Oh, sweetie, I threw it away.
What?!
Oprah's doctor friend said that teens who wear black fingernail polish are more likely to do drugs, so I--
Great! Now I have to mix all my *old* polish together and try to *make* black!
We're going to be late, aren't we?

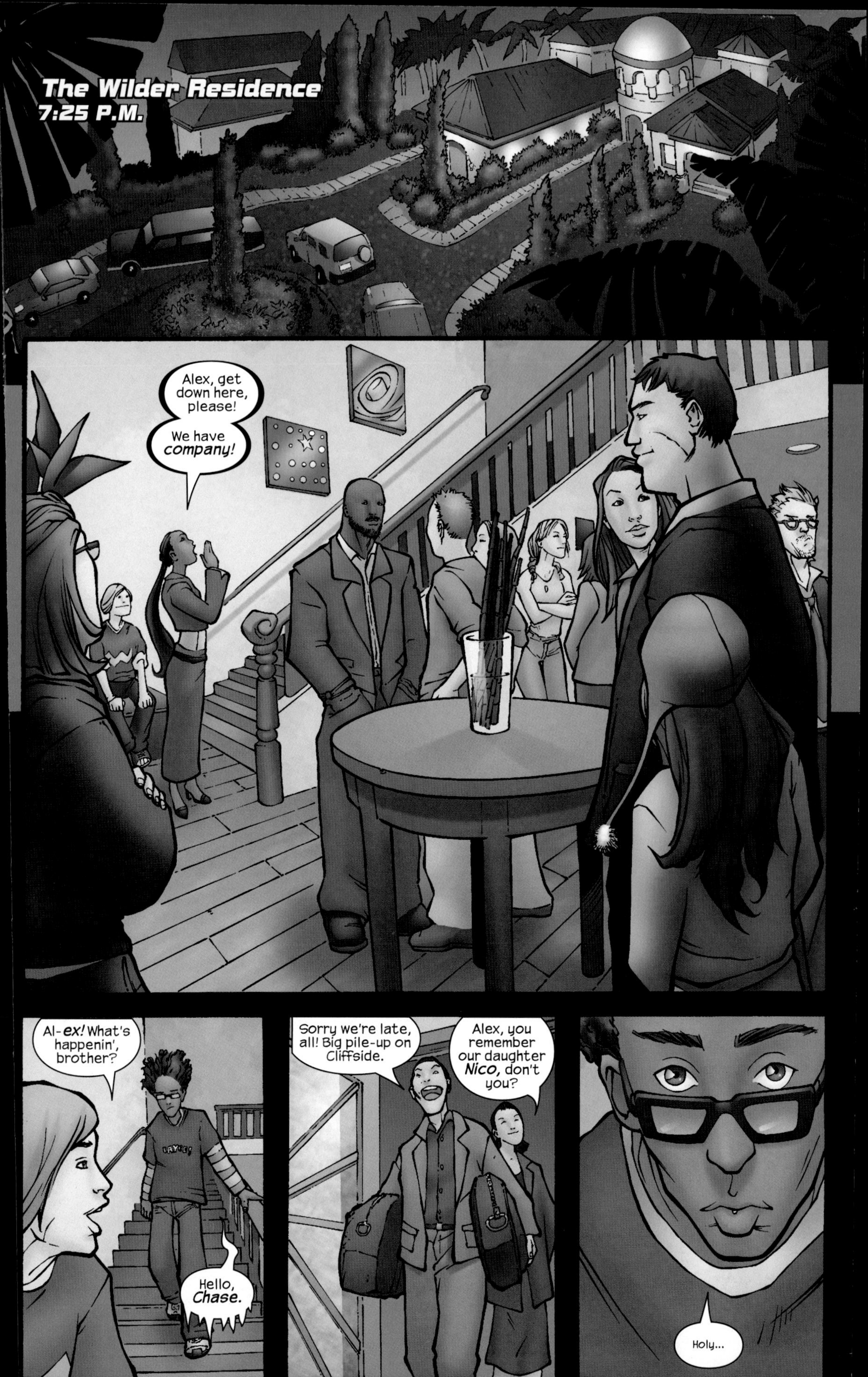
The Wilder Residence
7:25 P.M.
Alex, get down here, please!
We have company!
Al-ex! What's happenin', brother?
Hello, Chase.
Sorry we're late, all! Big pile-up on Cliffside.
Alex, you remember our daughter Nico, don't you?
Holy...

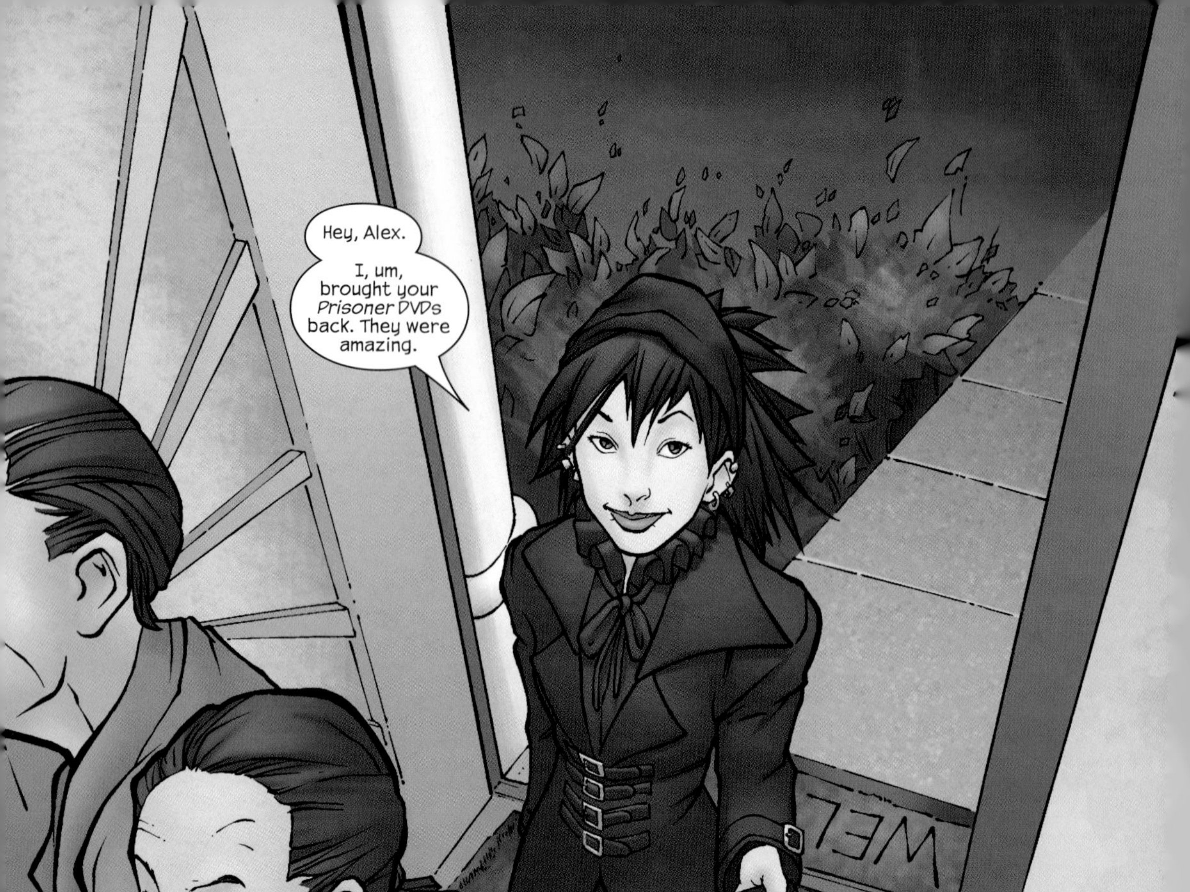

Hey, Alex.
I, um, brought your *Prisoner* DVDs back. They were amazing.
WEL
the Prisoner

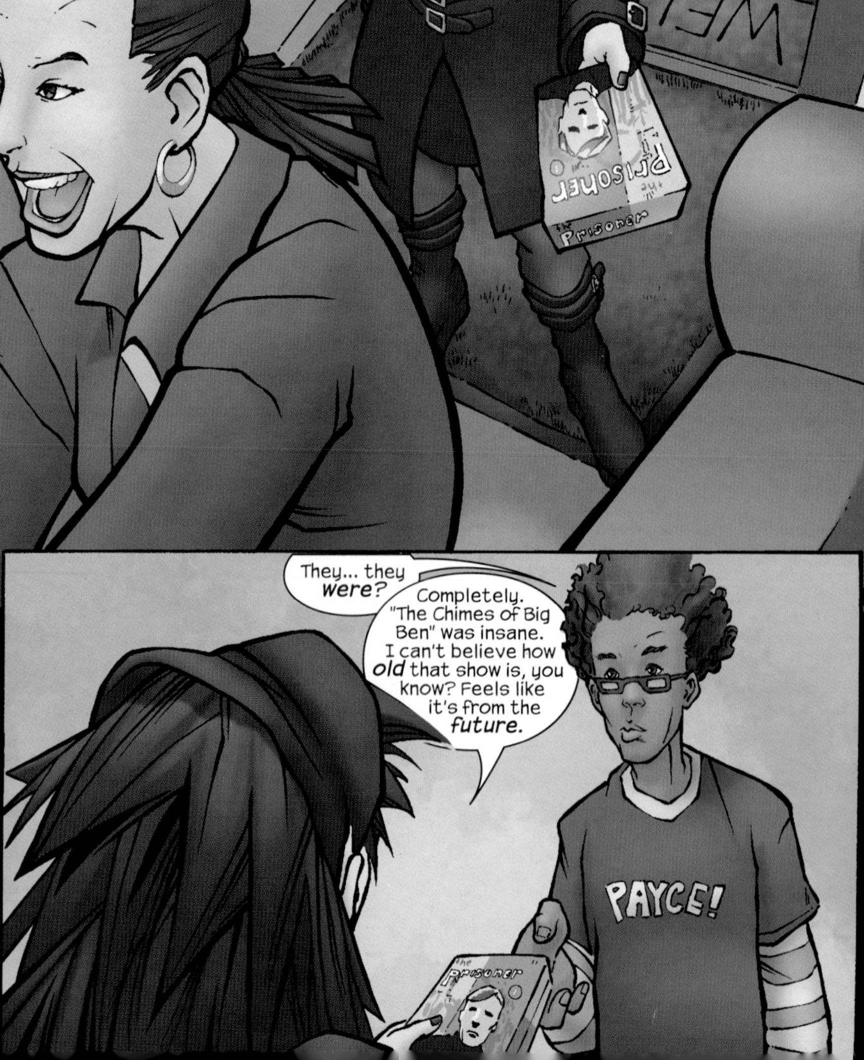

They... they *were*?
Completely. "The Chimes of Big Ben" was insane. I can't believe how *old* that show is, you know? Feels like it's from the *future.*
PAYCE!
the Prisoner

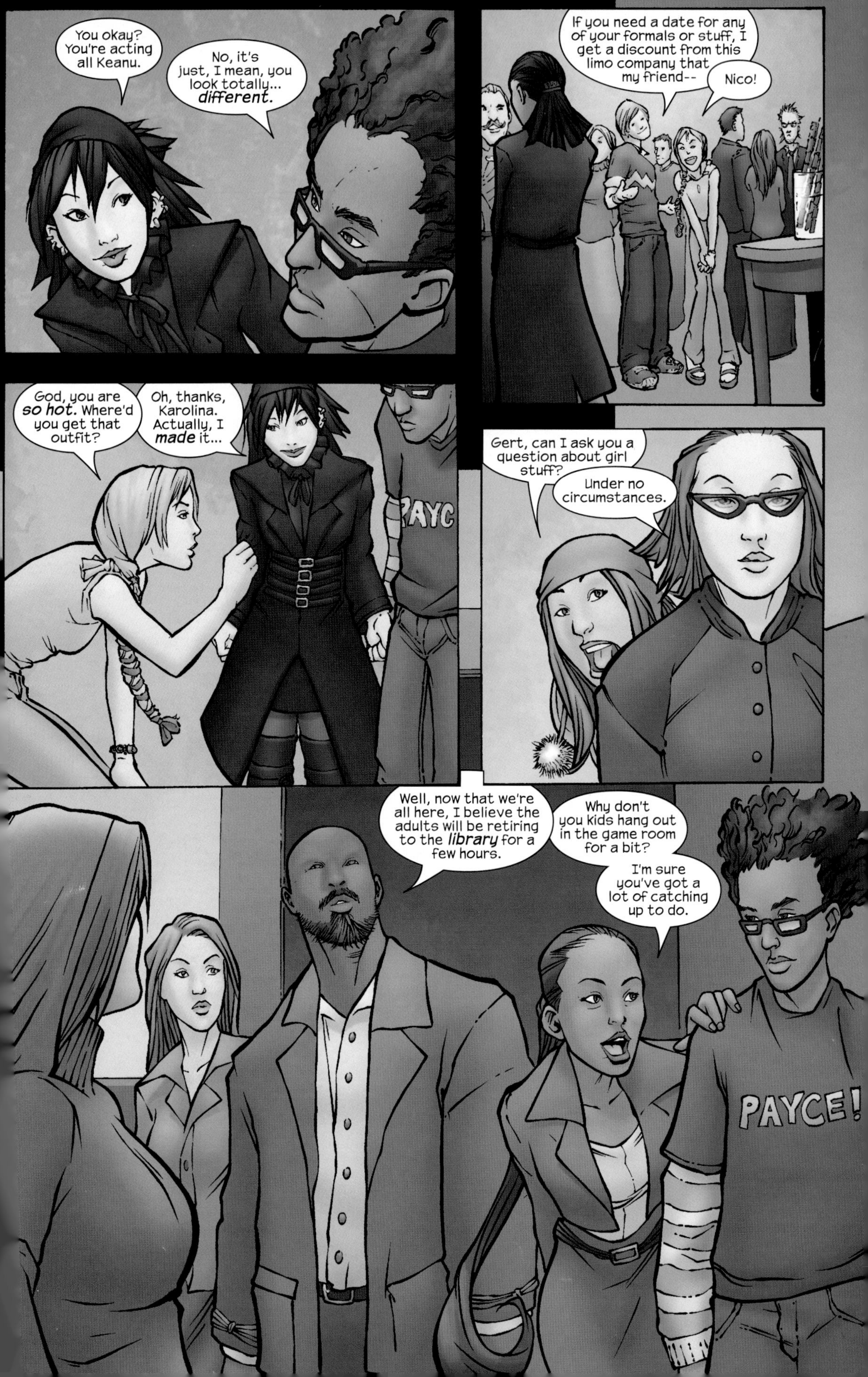
You okay? You're acting all Keanu.
No, it's just, I mean, you look totally... *different.*
If you need a date for any of your formals or stuff, I get a discount from this limo company that my friend--
Nico!
God, you are *so hot.* Where'd you get that outfit?
Oh, thanks, Karolina. Actually, I *made* it...
PAYC
Gert, can I ask you a question about girl stuff?
Under no circumstances.
Well, now that we're all here, I believe the adults will be retiring to the *library* for a few hours.
Why don't you kids hang out in the game room for a bit?
I'm sure you've got a lot of catching up to do.
PAYCE!

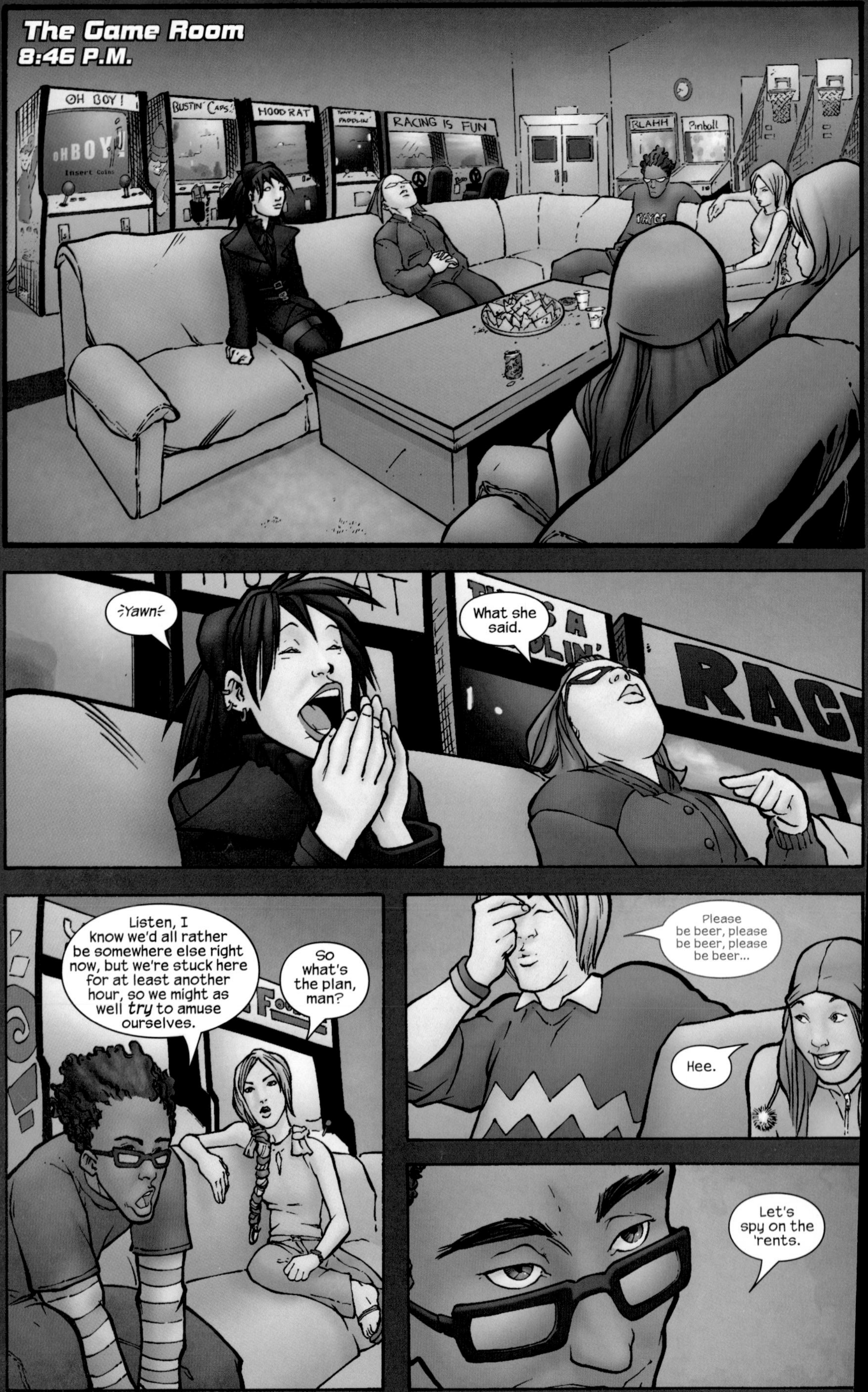
The Game Room
8:46 P.M.
OH BOY!
BUSTIN' CAPS!
HOOD RAT
RACING IS FUN
BLAHH
Pinball
OHBOY!
Insert Coins
Yawn
What she said.
RAC
Listen, I know we'd all rather be somewhere else right now, but we're stuck here for at least another hour, so we might as well *try* to amuse ourselves.
So what's the plan, man?
Please be beer, please be beer, please be beer...
Hee.
Let's spy on the 'rents.

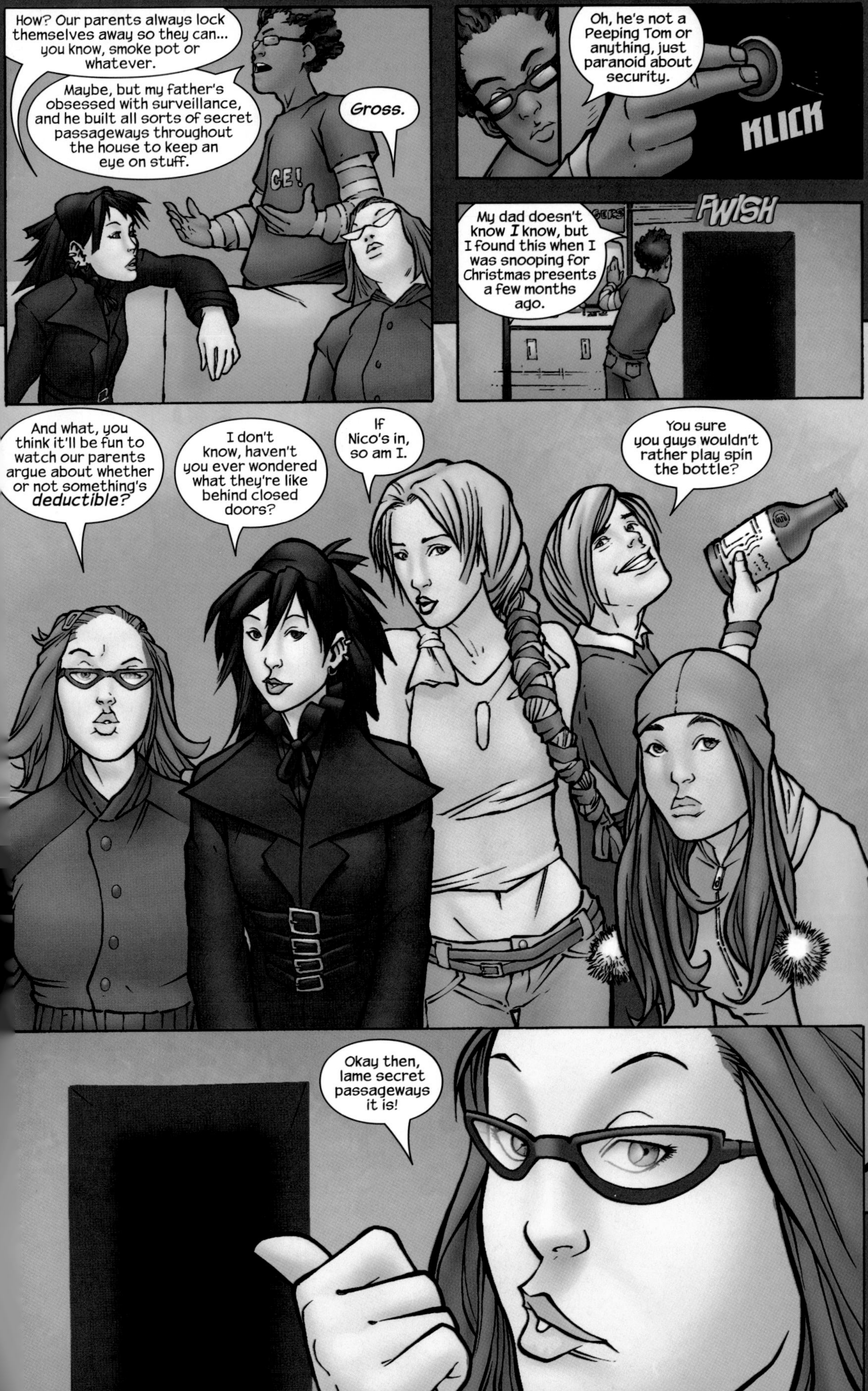
How? Our parents always lock themselves away so they can... you know, smoke pot or whatever.
Maybe, but my father's obsessed with surveillance, and he built all sorts of secret passageways throughout the house to keep an eye on stuff.
Gross.
CE!
Oh, he's not a Peeping Tom or anything, just paranoid about security.
KLICK
FWISH
My dad doesn't know *I* know, but I found this when I was snooping for Christmas presents a few months ago.
And what, you think it'll be fun to watch our parents argue about whether or not something's *deductible?*
I don't know, haven't you ever wondered what they're like behind closed doors?
If Nico's in, so am I.
You sure you guys wouldn't rather play spin the bottle?
Okay then, lame secret passageways it is!

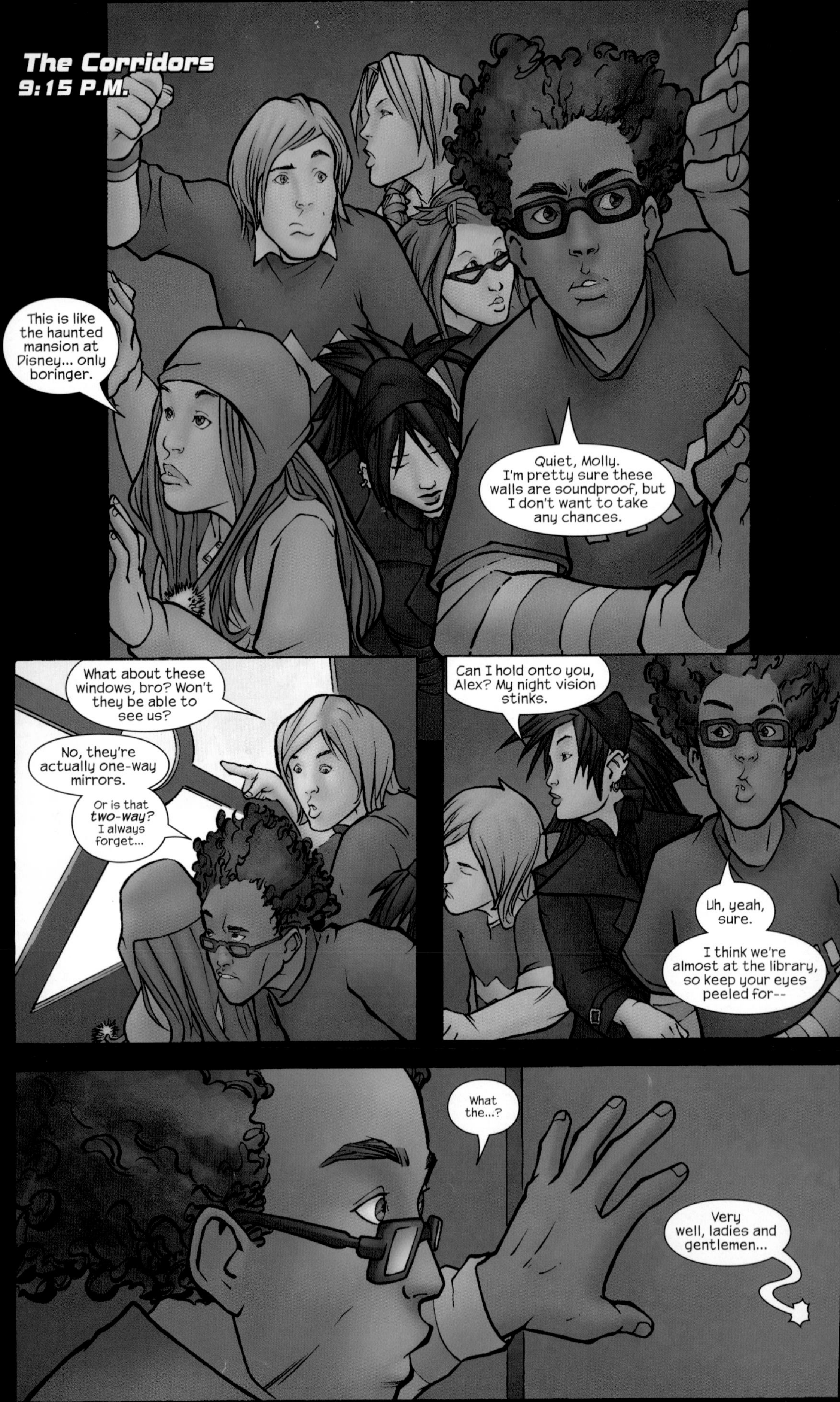
The Corridors
9:15 P.M.
This is like the haunted mansion at Disney... only boringer.
Quiet, Molly. I'm pretty sure these walls are soundproof, but I don't want to take any chances.
What about these windows, bro? Won't they be able to see us?
No, they're actually one-way mirrors.
Or is that *two-way*? I always forget...
Can I hold onto you, Alex? My night vision stinks.
Uh, yeah, sure.
I think we're almost at the library, so keep your eyes peeled for--
What the...?
Very well, ladies and gentlemen...

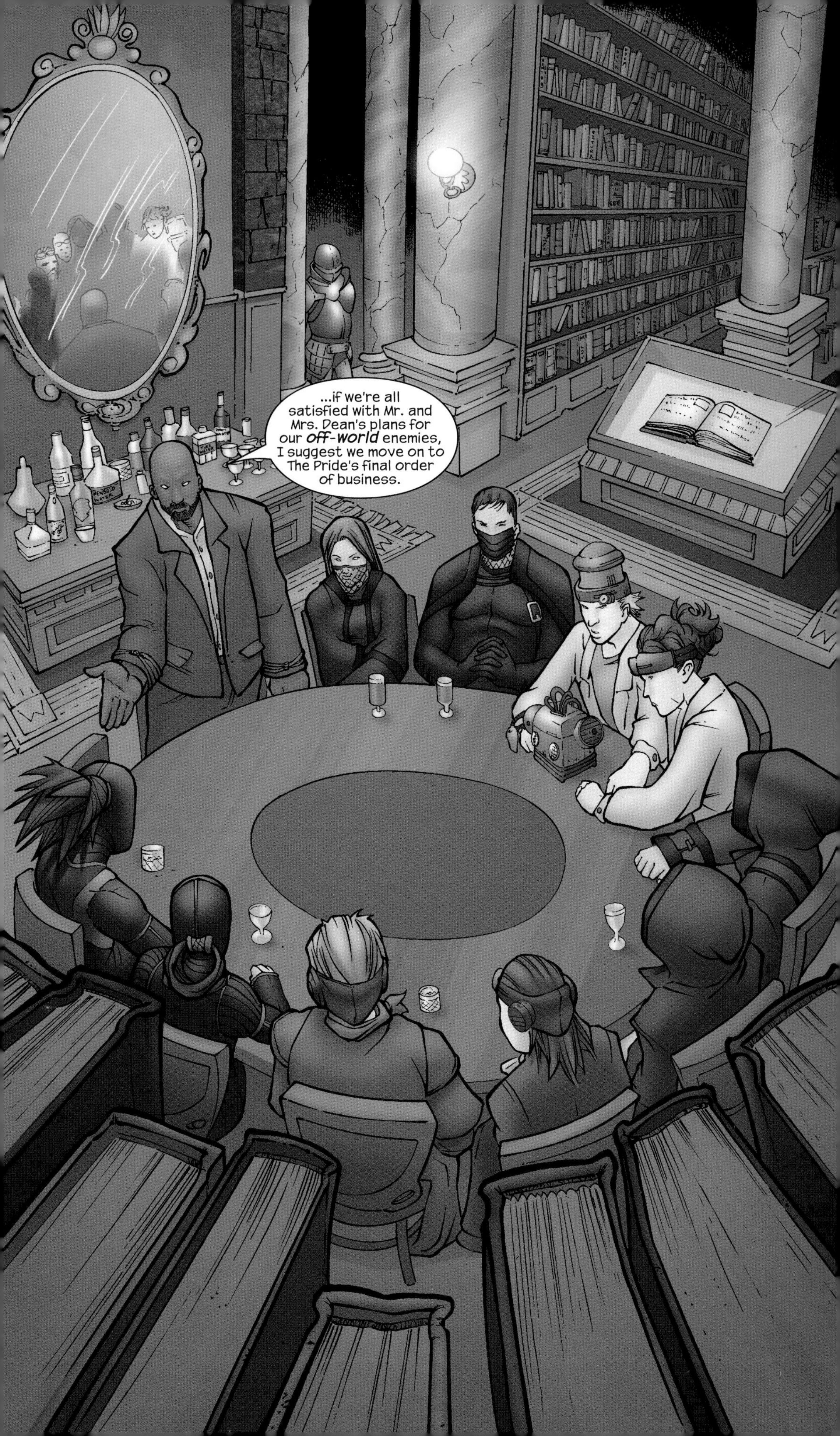
...if we're all satisfied with Mr. and Mrs. Dean's plans for our off-world enemies, I suggest we move on to The Pride's final order of business.

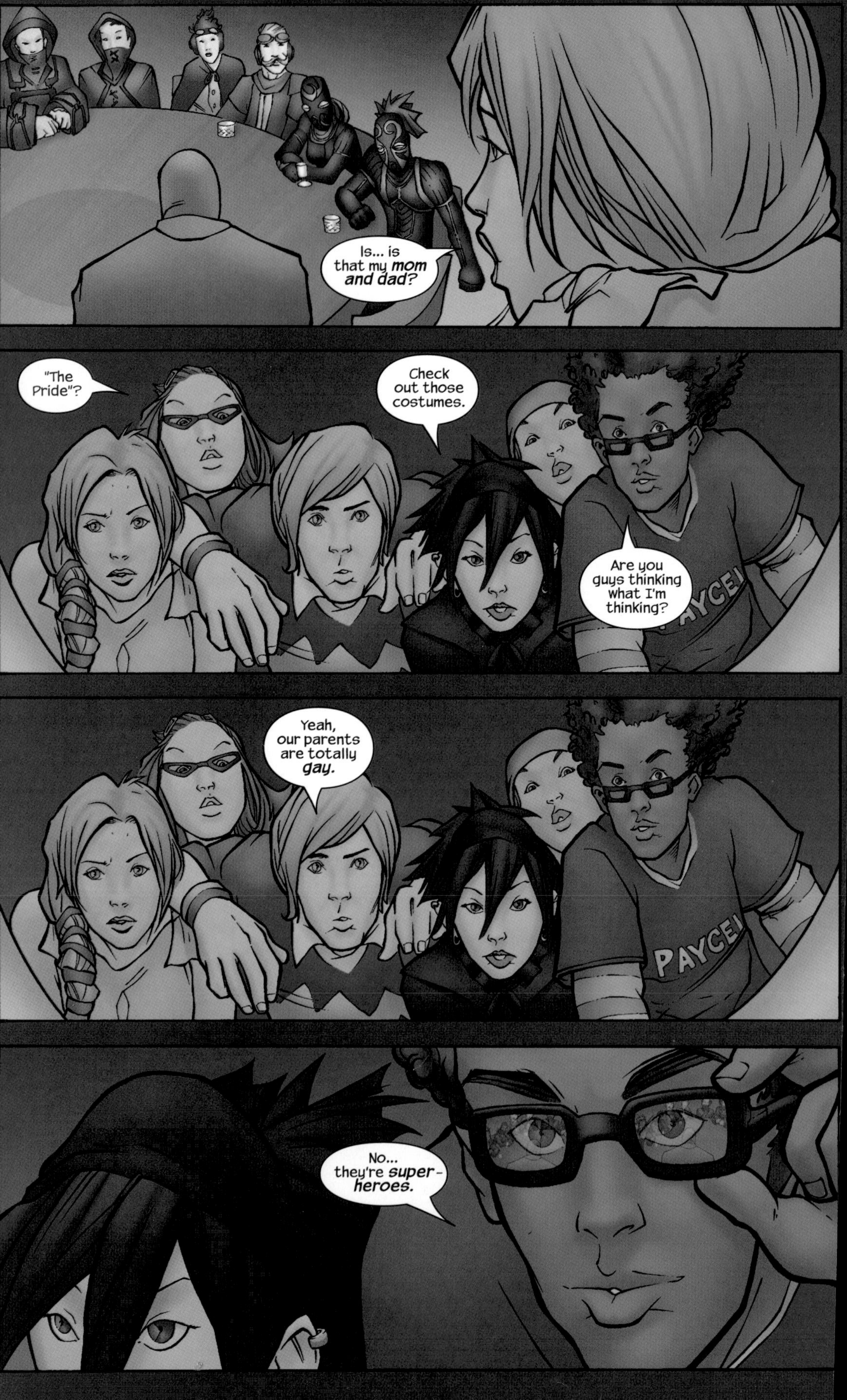

Is... is that my mom and dad?
"The Pride"?
Check out those costumes.
Are you guys thinking what I'm thinking?
PAYCE
Yeah, our parents are totally gay.
PAYCE
No... they're super-heroes.

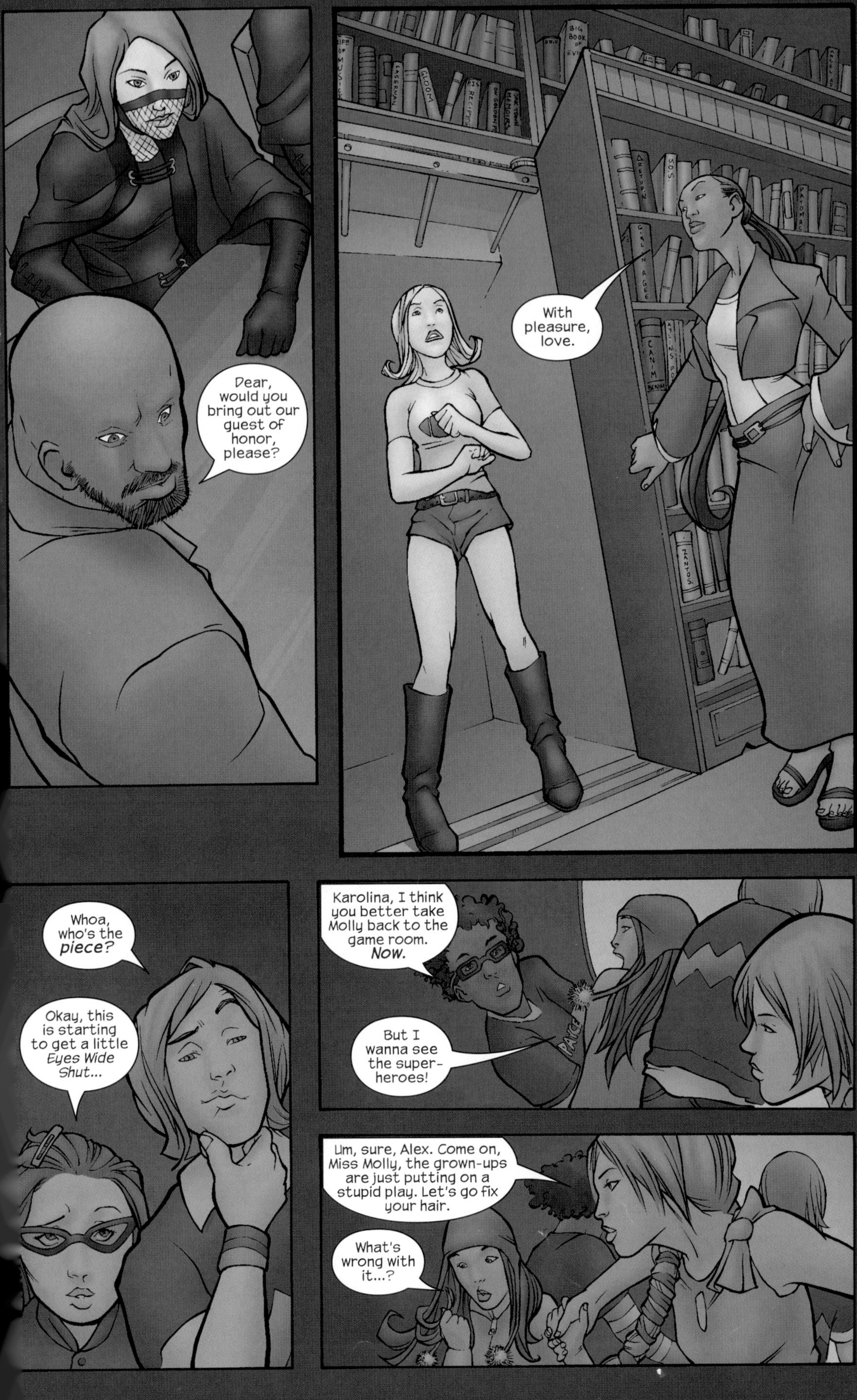
Dear, would you bring out our guest of honor, please?
With pleasure, love.
Whoa, who's the *piece?*
Okay, this is starting to get a little *Eyes Wide Shut...*
Karolina, I think you better take Molly back to the game room. **Now.**
But I wanna see the super-heroes!
Um, sure, Alex. Come on, Miss Molly, the grown-ups are just putting on a stupid play. Let's go fix your hair.
What's wrong with it...?

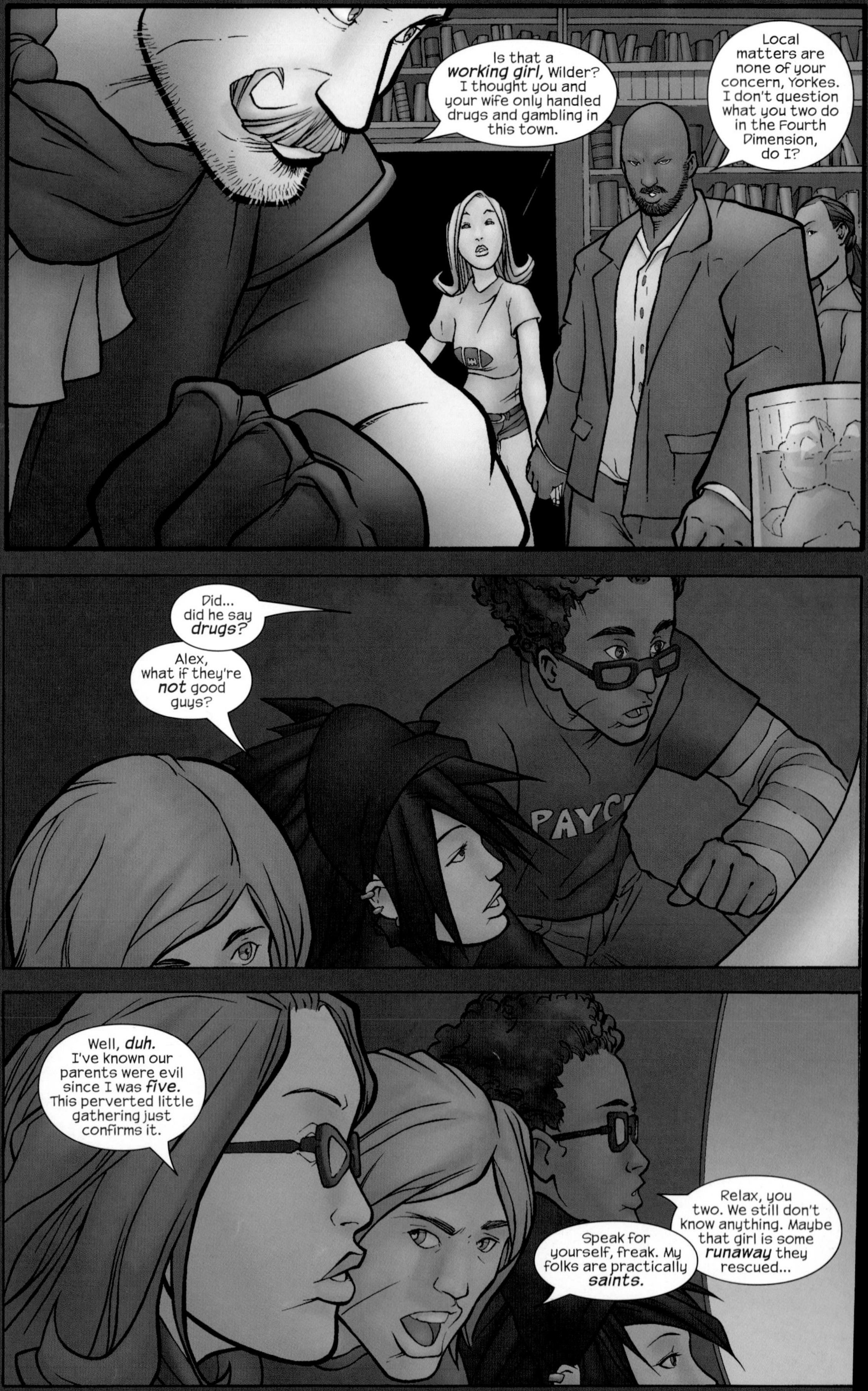
Is that a *working girl,* Wilder? I thought you and your wife only handled drugs and gambling in this town.
Local matters are none of your concern, Yorkes. I don't question what you two do in the Fourth Dimension, do I?
Did... did he say *drugs?*
Alex, what if they're *not* good guys?
Well, *duh.* I've known our parents were evil since I was *five.* This perverted little gathering just confirms it.
Relax, you two. We still don't know anything. Maybe that girl is some *runaway* they rescued...
Speak for yourself, freak. My folks are practically *saints.*

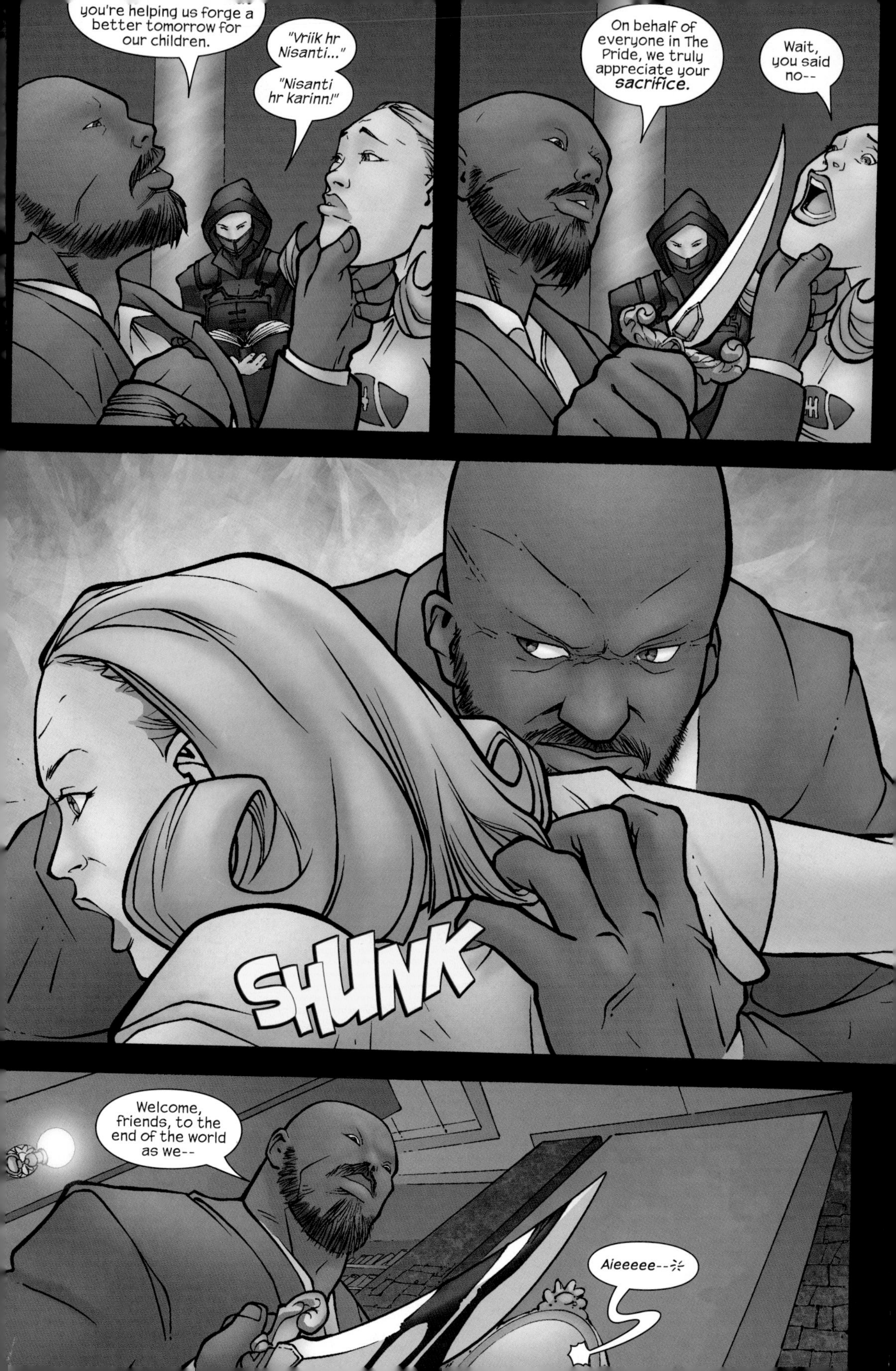

you're helping us forge a better tomorrow for our children.
"Vriik hr Nisanti..."
"Nisanti hr karinn!"
On behalf of everyone in The Pride, we truly appreciate your sacrifice.
Wait, you said no--
SHUNK
Welcome, friends, to the end of the world as we--
Aieeeee--

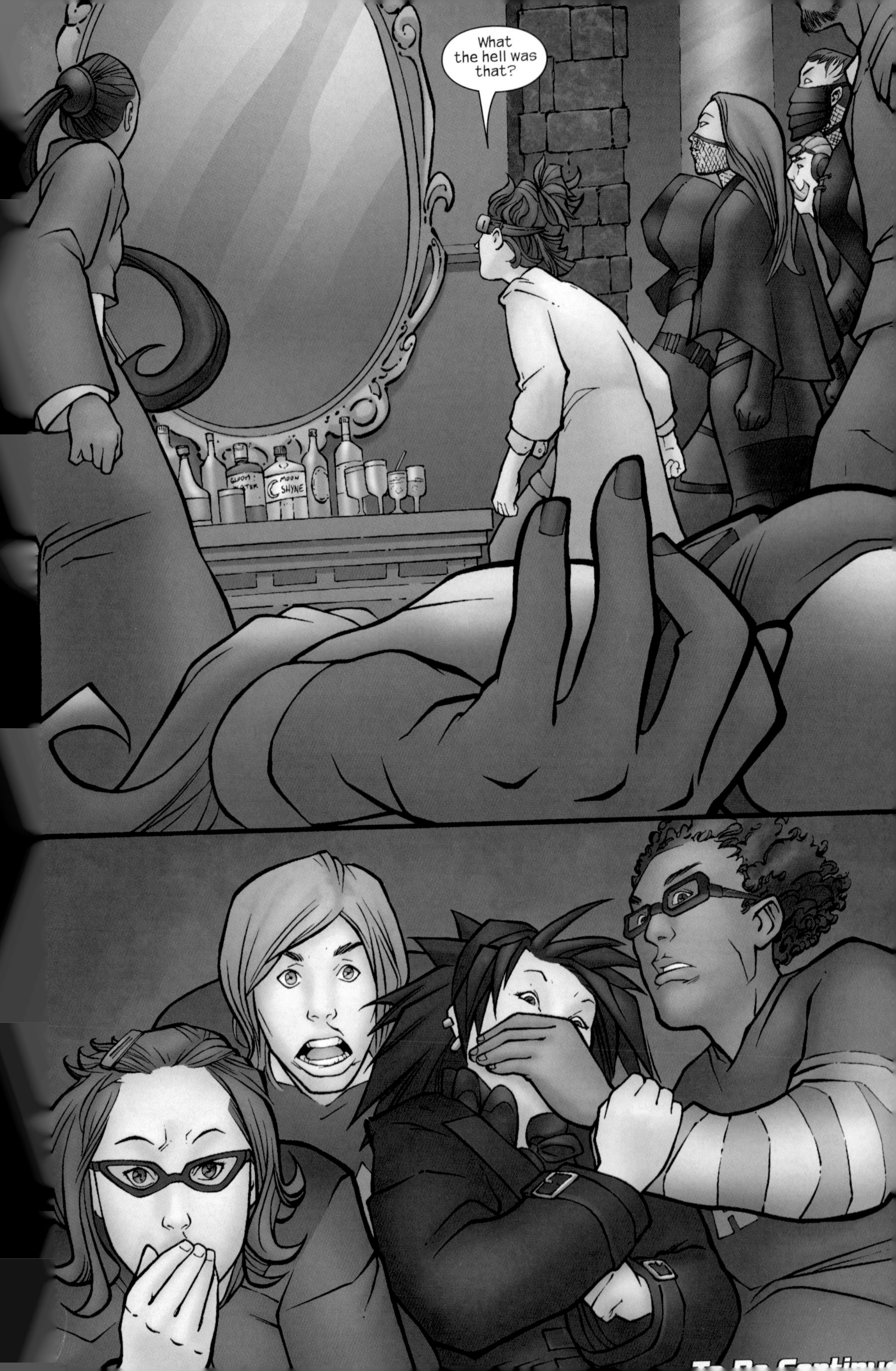
What the hell was that?
GLOOM
MOON SHYNE